# SYLVESTER ™
## and
## Tweety ™
## What a Mess!

By Gina Ingoglia

Illustrated by Bill Langley
and Vaccaro Assocs., Inc.

A Golden Book • New York
Western Publishing Company, Inc., Racine, Wisconsin 53404

Granny calls her cat.
"SYL-VES-TER!
SYL-VES-TER!
I will be back soon,"
she says.
"Do not make a mess."

3

Granny pets Tweety.
"Look out
for Sylvester,"
she says.

"Cats eat birds,"
says Granny.
"Sylvester is a cat.
YOU are a bird."

"Hello, Tweety,"
says Sylvester.
"Come out and play."

"No," says Tweety.
"I do not play
with cats.
I play with birds."

Sylvester thinks,
"I know what to do.

"Tweety will think
I am a bird."

"Hello, Tweety,"
says Sylvester.
"I am a bird.
Come out and play."

"Hello, bird,"
says Tweety.
"That will be fun!"

But look what
Tweety sees!
"He is not a bird!"
thinks Tweety.
"HE is a cat!

12

"I do not play
with cats,"
thinks Tweety.
"I know what to do!

14

"Bird," says Tweety,
"I will hide.
Come and find me."

"1-2-3-4-5!"
says Sylvester.

"Here I come!"
says Sylvester.
"Where are you?

"There you are!"
says Sylvester.
"Too bad, bird!"
says Tweety.
"What a mess!"

18

"1-2-3-4-5!"
says Sylvester.
"Here I come again!
Where are you?

"There you are!"
says Sylvester.
"Too bad, bird!"
says Tweety.
"What a mess!"

"1-2-3-4-5!
HERE I COME!"
says Sylvester.

"Where are you?"
says Sylvester.
"Where are you now?

"There you are!"
says Sylvester.

"Granny!" says Sylvester.
"Sylvester!" says Granny.

"What are you doing?"
says Granny.
"You are a cat,
not a bird!

"Look what you did!
What a bad cat
you are!"

"Too bad, bird!"
says Tweety.
"What a mess!"